DATE			